This Book Belongs To:

....

....

Stories for **Three** Year Olds

Stories for **Three** Year Olds

Bath · New York · Singapore · Hong Kong · Cologne · Delhi
Melbourne · Amsterdam · Johannesburg · Auckland · Shenzhen

Illustrated by Alison Atkins

First published by Parragon in 2011

Parragon
Queen Street House
4 Queen Street
Bath BA1 1HE, UK

Copyright © Parragon Books Ltd 2003

ISBN 978-1-4454-1987-9

Printed in China

Contents

Poor Humphrey

Humphrey was a baby rhino and he wasn't at all happy. He had a bumpy thing on his face instead of a spike, and he didn't like it at all.

So Humphrey refused to go out unless he was wearing a cardboard box to cover it.

"How can I wash behind your ears, you silly thing?" Mom would laugh when she tried to give him a bath. And if he got a cold and tried to blow his nose, well—you've never seen such a mess!

One day, Humphrey was fed up staying indoors. He just had to go outside.

He stumbled along trying to look at things through the holes in his box. He saw a lizard on a rock. He sniffed a red flower on a bush. He watched an army of ants carrying things on their backs.

Suddenly, Humphrey heard giggling. He felt a tug at his box.

"Hey!" he shouted. "Give that back Monkey."

Humphrey was angry. He put the box back on his head. Then he heard singing and laughing. It instantly cheered him up.

Into the clearing came a group of baby rhinos. And guess what! They were all wearing cardboard boxes on their heads, just like Humphrey. They stopped when they saw him and asked him to play with them.

Humphrey stayed in the clearing all afternoon, playing games, singing songs, and telling rhino jokes.

One day not long after, Humphrey put on his best box to go out. When he did this, it ripped right down the front. He felt the front of his face. There was something there. Something sharp.

He went to the water's edge and looked at his reflection. Wow! There it was, plain as the nose on your face. The "bumpy thing" had gone and Humphrey had a beautiful pointy spike.

"From now on, my name is Spike," said Humphrey proudly. And off he went, without his box, to meet his new friends.

And do you know what? They weren't wearing boxes any more, either!

The Remembering Fairy

Georgina's mom was very forgetful. Every day she would forget something important. Sometimes, she even forgot to wake Georgina up!

One particular day, Georgina was feeling very miserable. Mom had forgotten that today there was a costume party at school, and had not made Georgina a costume.

The other children came to preschool dressed as clowns and ballerinas, or as wild animals and monsters.

Georgina was just wearing normal clothes!

"I wish there was a way I could make Mom remember things," she said sadly.

Suddenly, there was a puff of smoke and sparkle.

"I'm the Remembering Fairy," said a little voice, "and I'm here to help."

"But how can you help?" asked Georgina, feeling very confused.

"I help people like your mom remember things," said the fairy. "So, next time your mom is about to forget something, I'll be there!"

"Thank you," said Georgina.

The fairy smiled, and disappeared in another puff of smoke and sparkle.

"Well," thought Georgina, "what a helpful fairy."

The next morning, Georgina came down to breakfast. She was surprised to see Mom waiting for her with her lunch box already packed.

The next few days were the same. Every time Mom had something important to remember, the Remembering Fairy popped up and whispered in her ear.

After two weeks with the Remembering Fairy, Georgina's mom found she was starting to remember things more and more.

"You know," said Mom, "I really think my memory is getting much better."

Georgina heard a familiar puff of smoke and sparkle near her ear.

"Well, Georgina," whispered the fairy, "I think my job here is done."

Georgina smiled. "Mom does seem really good at remembering things now. Thank you so much, Fairy."

"I'm very happy to help," said the fairy, and in a flash she was gone.

Georgina hasn't seen the fairy again since, but she always keeps an eye out for that special puff of smoke and sparkle— she certainly won't forget the Remembering Fairy!

The Selfish Puppy

Everyone adored Bonnie. She was the biggest, prettiest, smartest puppy in the litter. Wherever she went everyone fussed over her.

However, Bonnie was also very selfish.

"Move out of the way," she would bark at dinnertime, as she pushed past the smaller puppies.

When it came to bedtime, she always made sure that she got the comfiest spot beside the fire.

And, worst of all, she would never let the other puppies play with the toys.

Her behavior made the other puppies angry.

One day, after Bonnie had eaten all the food without offering them so much as a bite, they were madder than ever.

They decided to ignore Bonnie to teach her a lesson.

After a while, Bonnie started to feel lonely, so she went to find her brothers. They were playing with a ball.

"Play with me," she said. But the other puppies ran off.

Later, she found them cuddling up next to their mother and father.

"Mom, Dad," whined Bonnie. "They won't play with me. It's not fair. After all, I am a SPECIAL puppy."

"Oh, dear," said her mother. "I think it's about time we had a little talk. You are very special," she began, "but so are Bill, Ben, and Titch," said her mother.

Bonnie looked shocked.

"But they won't play with me," she whined.

"Well," said her mother. "Have you been playing nicely with them? Have you been sharing things?"

"Well...no," whispered Bonnie.

Her mother shook her head sadly. "Perhaps you should try sharing things, then you might find that your brothers will want to play with you."

"Really," whispered Bonnie, looking doubtfully at the other puppies.

Bill, Ben, and Titch wagged their tails.

"And you never know," added her father. "You might even discover that sharing things is fun!"

Bonnie wasn't at all sure about this sharing thing.

But the next morning, she made sure that each puppy had an equal share of food. And in the afternoon she showed them her secret stash of bones.

Bill, Ben, and Titch were so happy.

Later that night, all four of them curled up together in front of the fire.

"You were right," smiled Bonnie, turning to her parents. "Sharing really is fun."

Smile, please!

One morning, the family decided to have a family photo taken as a birthday present for Grandma.

That weekend, they all put on their best clothes. It wasn't long before Mr. Toogood, the photographer, arrived and set up a lot of special lights in the living room. He asked everyone to take their places.

Everyone smiled for the camera…except Josie.

"Smile, please, Josie," Mr. Toogood said.

"But this isn't all of our family," said Josie and ran off to get Snuffles, her hamster.

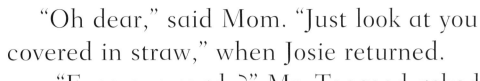

"Oh dear," said Mom. "Just look at you covered in straw," when Josie returned.

"Everyone ready?" Mr. Toogood asked as they posed again. They all nodded… except Josie.

"I want Wilbur in the photo," she said. Wilbur was the family cat.

"Meow!" wailed Wilbur, as Josie carried him back to the sofa.

"Everyone ready?" asked Mr. Toogood. "Smile, please!"

"Just a minute," said Josie. "It won't be right without Cuddles." Cuddles was Josie's favorite teddy bear.

"Make it fast!" said Mom.

Josie finally found Cuddles under her bed.

"Okay. Here we go, at last," said Mom, trying to stay calm.

Josie took her place on the sofa, hugging Cuddles. Wilbur purred on Mom's lap. Snuffles slept in Danny's arms. Everyone began to smile...except Josie. A big tear began to trickle down her cheek.

"Oh dear," said Mr. Toogood.

"What's the matter?" asked Dad.

"Grandma will be sad if Jumble isn't in the picture. She loves Jumble."

It was true. Grandma did love their dog, Jumble. But no one remembered seeing him all morning. Everyone shouted his name. Then they waited.

There was a pattering sound in the hall and Jumble dashed into the living room.

His paws were covered in dirt and his fur was very messy. He had a bone in his mouth. He jumped up onto Danny. All the other animals jumped up too!

"Woof!" Jumbles barked, as he landed on Dad's lap. He wagged his tail in Dad's face.

"Smile, PLEASE!" shouted Mr. Toogood.

And Josie smiled. Everyone else burst out laughing. Mr. Toogood pressed the button on his camera.

"At last!" he said.

"What will Grandma think?" asked Mom.

"Grandma will love it," said Josie.

And Josie was right. Grandma did love the picture. It made her smile too.

The Very Serious Lion Cub

Bantu was a very serious little lion cub. He never smiled and he never ever laughed. You see, Bantu was the son of Addo, King of the Jungle, and he knew that one day he, too, would become king. And the thought of following in his father's HUGE footsteps worried Bantu.

King Addo tried his best to bring a smile to his son's face, but nothing worked.

Then, one day, King Addo decided that enough was enough. He called a jungle meeting.

"Tomorrow we're going to have a contest," he announced. "A contest to make my son, Bantu, laugh. Whoever makes him laugh first, will be made king for a day."

The jungle animals gasped. Then they started to chatter excitedly among themselves.

The following afternoon, everyone met beside the watering hole. A miserable looking Bantu sat beside his father as the other animals tried to get his attention.

The hefty hippos stumbled and bumbled their way through a hilarious ballet. Everyone watched Bantu, but his lips didn't so much as twitch.

Next to take the stage were the amazing miming chimpanzees, whose speciality was doing imitations of other jungle animals.

After the chimpanzees came the laughing hyenas, followed by the wrestling rhinos and the gyrating giraffes.

But none of the acts brought so much as a smile to Bantu's lips.

As the last giraffe waltzed off the stage, King Addo rose sadly.

"I would like to thank you all," he sighed, as he paced up and down. "But it would appear that nothing can make my little Bantu laugh."

King Addo hadn't noticed the banana peel that had been dropped in his way.

"Watch out," cried Bantu, as King Addo slipped off the bank. But he was too late.

"Ahhhhhh," roared King Addo, as he skidded on the banana peel and landed in the watering hole.

"Oooooh," gasped Bantu. Then his lips began to twitch, and his chin began to wobble. Then, much to King Addo's amazement, Bantu began to laugh.

The laughing got louder and louder, until, before long, he was rolling around on the ground.

"S...s...sorry, Dad," he hiccuped. "But you just look sooooo funny. Perhaps following in your footsteps won't be so difficult, after all."